The Rescue Princesses

The Lost Gold

More amazing animal adventures!

The Secret Promise

The Wishing Pearl

The Moonlight Mystery

The Stolen Crystals

The Snow Jewel

The Magic Rings

The Rescue Princesses

The Lost Gold

💜 PAULA HARRISON 💜

Scholastic Inc.

For Leni and Hester

ISBN 978-0-545-50920-6

Text copyright © 2013 by Paula Harrison
Interior illustrations copyright © 2013 by Artful Doodlers

All rights reserved. Published by Scholastic Inc., 557 Broadway, New York, NY 10012, by arrangement with Nosy Crow Ltd.

12 11 10 9 8 7 6 5 4 3 2 1   13 14 15 16 17 18/0

Printed in the U.S.A.   40
First printing, December 2013

CHAPTER ONE

The Blue Butterfly

Princess Isabella crept through the rain forest with a small monkey riding on her shoulder. Parrots squawked to one another in the treetops and water drops from the last rain shower glinted on the broad leaves.

Isabella's curly brown hair was loosely tied with a ribbon and determinaton shone in her dark eyes. The butterfly that she was following had landed on a leaf and was flexing its beautiful wings. She held her breath and lifted up her camera slowly. It looked so perfect. The shiny wings were sky blue with velvety black edges. She'd been trying to take a photo of a Blue Morpho butterfly for weeks and this was her chance!

"Stay really still, Petro," she whispered to the monkey. "This will make a great picture!"

She peered at the screen, holding her finger just above the button. The butterfly looked very small. If only she could get a little closer. She took a tiny step toward it, but her foot caught on a tree root and she stumbled. She grabbed a branch to catch herself, but it snapped. Petro leapt off her shoulder, chattering angrily, and Isabella landed on the ground on her hands and knees.

Disturbed by the noise, the blue butterfly

flew into the treetops, its wings shimmering in the dappled sunlight.

"Oh no!" Isabella watched it go before searching the ground for the camera she'd dropped. She found it and stood up, brushing the earth from her cherry-red dress. Petro ran along a branch, still chattering.

"I'm sorry, Petro!" Isabella checked the camera for scratches. "I thought I was getting better. I've been practicing ninja moves every day, but I'm still no good!" She sighed heavily. "I walk into things and trip just as much as before."

Petro leapt gracefully down to her shoulder and nuzzled her ear. His soft tail curled lovingly around her neck.

"Thanks! You always cheer me up." Isabella smiled at the little brown monkey. She thought for a moment about her three new princess friends and how they had all promised to work on their ninja moves and other rescue skills. Well, she would just have to keep practicing!

She had met Princesses Lottie, Amina, and Rosalind a few weeks ago at a royal dance festival. They'd decided to call themselves the Rescue Princesses and help animals in danger, just like Lottie's older sister and her friends used to do.

They'd had an amazing adventure at the festival, saving some horses and a beautiful foal from being stolen. They had all become good friends, too. Now that Isabella was back home in the kingdom of Belatina, she missed the other princesses a lot.

She smiled at Petro. "Maybe another butterfly will come past before we have to go back for lunch."

She glanced at the tall towers of the palace behind her and then stepped deeper into the rain forest. Petro leapt off her shoulder and swung from tree to tree behind her. They often took walks here together. Isabella had found Petro alone in the forest when he was only a baby. She had taken him back home and cared for him, saving fruit from her meals to feed him. When he was older, she'd thought that he would want to live in the wild again, but he had refused to go. They had been best friends ever since.

Isabella stopped to look at a toucan with a huge golden beak, perching on a branch above her. This would make a good photo. She rested one hand on the thick tree trunk while she reached for her camera.

Suddenly, she froze. A sharp banging shattered the peace of the forest, and the tree trunk trembled under her fingers.

"What's that, Petro?" she said. "I haven't heard that noise before."

Petro's quick eyes darted all around and he ran back and forth along his branch.

After a few moments, the banging happened again. It was louder this time and was followed by a high-pitched grinding sound that made Isabella shudder. Petro leapt back onto her shoulder and put his hands over his ears.

"Poor Petro!" said Isabella, stroking his soft, furry head. "I know you hate loud noises, but we have to find out what it is."

She hurried toward the sound, searching for what it could be. At last she saw something through the trees. Creeping forward, she hid behind a tree trunk, her heart beating faster and faster. There was a group of men standing in the middle of a clearing.

Isabella frowned. What were they doing? She hardly ever saw people in this part of the forest, and never so many at the same time. Where had the clearing come from? She was sure there had been thick forest here before.

One of the men began to use a metal saw to cut a tree. The grinding noise grew louder as the saw bit into the trunk. The tree started to sway and, very slowly, it toppled over and crashed to the ground.

Isabella gasped. That was what the sounds were. They were cutting down the trees! She noticed several more fallen trees stacked to one side. This was terrible! The trees provided shelter and food for so many rain-forest creatures.

These men had to be stopped. Should she go and tell them what they were doing was wrong? Just then, a small brown shape sprang out of a nearby tree and scampered across the clearing. It was a wild forest monkey and it looked very frightened. A bunch of yellow fruit

fell to the ground. Isabella knew why the monkey had been up the tree. Those fruits were their favorite food.

"Hey!" yelled one of the men. "Get out of here!" He ran toward the monkey, chasing it away.

Petro gave a squeak of fright and his little hands dug into Isabella's shoulders. Isabella felt so angry with the man she thought she might burst.

"Don't worry, Petro," she whispered. "We'll go back to the palace right now. Once my mom and dad find out what's going on, they'll tell these terrible men to leave the forest alone." She took one last look. One of the men was staring curiously in their direction.

Isabella stayed completely still until he'd turned away again. "Stay in the shadows," she told Petro. "And let's run!"

CHAPTER TWO

The Legend of the Lost Gold

Isabella raced through the rain forest as quietly as she could. Petro moved from branch to branch, swinging through the treetops, so he reached the palace grounds first. Hanging by his tail from the top of the silver gate, he waited for Isabella to catch up.

"I'm here, Petro," Isabella gasped after sprinting through the gate and up the path. Her cherry-red dress swirled out behind her and the ribbon escaped from her curly brown hair and blew away in the breeze. Petro jumped down and galloped after her.

The palace of Belatina was made of gleaming white stone. At the front, a row of towering pillars reached up to a triangular-shaped roof. Isabella ran past the long flower beds and up the broad stone steps to the front entrance. Ignoring the surprised looks of the guards at the front door, she dashed through the hallway and into the dining room to find her parents.

She skidded to a halt in front of them. Petro ran in behind her and jumped onto her shoulder.

"Mom! Dad!" she said breathlessly. "Something awful has happened! Some men are cutting down trees in the rain forest. Please come and stop them!"

Isabella paused to take a breath, and

realized that her parents didn't look as alarmed as she'd expected them to.

"Slow down, Isabella, and tell us calmly what is the matter." Her mom, Queen Neva, poured herself a glass of pineapple juice. With her long brown hair and brown eyes, she looked just like her daughter.

Isabella took another breath. She noticed that her dad was staring at a piece of paper and hadn't even looked up. "Please, Dad! I need you to stop these men before they cut down too many trees."

"What's that?" Her dad finally looked at her. "Did you see some men working in the forest?"

Isabella nodded. She glanced at the piece of paper in her dad's hand. It was flecked with brown and crinkled at the edges.

"They're a group of treasure hunters, Isabella." King Victor rolled up the paper and fastened it with an elastic band. "You must keep out of their way. They have important work to do."

Isabella stared at him in astonishment. "But, Dad —" she began.

"You've heard of the legend of the lost gold, haven't you?" The king reached up to straighten his heavy crown. "It's a very famous story after all."

"You know, dear. I used to tell you that story at bedtime when you were little," said Queen Neva.

"Oh! Yes, the lost gold. It's a good story," said Isabella. "But —"

"But it's NOT just a story!" said the king triumphantly. "The gold belonged to people who lived in our rain forest over a hundred years ago. So many people tried to steal it that they hid the treasure away.

Time went by and the gold was lost, but now we have a chance to find it again!"

Petro sprang lightly onto the table and began sorting through the oranges and mangoes while no one was paying attention.

The king held up the mysterious roll of paper, a dreamy look in his eyes. "This is the famous Silken Scroll, which has been kept safe in our palace for many years! It contains a secret code that tells where the gold is hidden. The treasure hunters have cracked the code. The legend says when the lost treasure is found, it will bring good luck and happiness to the whole kingdom."

"But what will we do with the treasure?" asked Isabella.

"Do with it?" The king frowned. "Well, keep it of course! In fact, the treasure

hunters have offered me half of everything they find!"

"But, Dad! What about the trees?" cried Isabella.

"Maybe they need to cut down a few trees so that they can dig in the right place." The king noticed Petro on the table. "Get that monkey off the table AT ONCE! That pet should not be in here at all. This is a royal dining room, not a zoo!"

Isabella leaned across, trying to get ahold of Petro, but her arm knocked over the glass pitcher and pineapple juice went splashing all over her mom.

"Isabella!" shrieked the queen, dabbing at her dress with a napkin.

Her screech made Petro jump, and he galloped across the table, knocking over the fruit bowl. Then he scampered out the door.

"Sorry! I didn't mean to! I was just trying to grab Petro." Isabella set the pitcher upright and started putting the fruit back into the bowl.

King Victor rose from his chair. "I'm going to put the Silken Scroll away in my desk before anything gets spilled on it."

"I'm really sorry about Petro getting on the table, Dad," said Isabella. "But please think about the trees! What will the monkeys do if these men cut down too many of their favorite fruit trees? It will be hard for them to find food."

The king looked down his long nose. "I know you want to help, Isabella. But the monkeys have plenty of other trees to choose from." He swept out of the room, taking the rolled-up scroll with him.

CHAPTER THREE

The Jewels of Belatina

Isabella found Petro hiding behind a large, brightly painted vase at the top of the stairs. "It's all right, Petro. It was really me that my dad was angry with." She sighed. "I wish he understood about the trees. It's not just the monkeys that live in them. There are tree frogs and lizards, parrots and toucans, and so many other creatures."

Petro crept out from behind the vase

and nuzzled her hand before springing
up onto her shoulder.

"Isabella?" called Queen Neva. "Can
you come here for a moment?"

Isabella found her mom sitting in front
of the vanity mirror in her bedroom,
fastening an earring onto each ear.

"I know you're disappointed about
the trees," said the queen. "But I don't
think they'll cut down very many."

"The thing is that each tree provides
food and shelter to a lot of animals," said
Isabella. "I wish they didn't have to hunt
for the gold."

"Finding olden-day treasure helps us
to learn more about our country's past,"
said the queen, opening her green velvet
jewelry box. "All royal jewels have a
story behind them. Soon I will teach you
more about our crowns, necklaces, and

brooches, and where each one comes from." She took out a hair clip in the shape of a butterfly with wings made from gleaming sapphires. "This would look wonderful on you! Your hair does need taming, as you seem to have lost your hair ribbon. Would you like to try it on?"

Isabella tried to smile. "No, I . . . just don't really feel like it right now." She stared out the window. In the distance she could see the palace wall, and beyond that the forest.

Petro jumped lightly onto the vanity table and began sorting through the jewelry box. He picked up the butterfly hair clip, which looked huge in his little hands. He gazed at its sparkling blue surface.

"I know you're worried about the rain forest, but can't we do something to take your mind off it?" asked Queen Neva.

Isabella opened her mouth to say that nothing would take her mind off the trees and the rain-forest creatures she loved so much. But then a thought popped into her head. It was such an amazing idea that it made her eyes sparkle and her stomach flip over. She wasn't getting anywhere trying to protect the rain forest by herself, but maybe if she had some help it would be easier.

"Mom?" she said carefully. "I met some other princesses when we went to the dance festival in the kingdom of Peronia and I'd love to see them again. Can they come visit?"

Queen Neva scanned her face and then smiled. "What a good idea! That's just what you need — some other girls to do princess things with!"

Isabella tried very hard to keep a straight face. Her mom didn't know that she and her friends were more interested in rescuing animals than anything else!

"What are your friends' names?" asked the queen. "I'll send them a royal invitation right away!"

"Thanks, Mom!" Isabella beamed. "There's Princess Lottie. She's from the kingdom of Middingland. Then Princess Amina is from the kingdom of Kamala by the eastern sea, and Princess Rosalind comes from Dalvia in the far north."

Her mom took a piece of paper out of a drawer and wrote down the names. "I will contact their parents today. Why don't you go and tell Cook that we might be having visitors. We will certainly need to have a special banquet to welcome them."

"I'll go right now!" Isabella hugged her mom. "Come on, Petro! Let's go and find Cook."

Petro managed to lift the blue butterfly hair clip up and put it on top of his head. He chattered to his reflection in the mirror, as if he thought he looked very pretty.

Isabella giggled. "Oh, Petro! You can't keep that, you know! It belongs in the jewelry box."

She gently took the sapphire hair clip from his fingers and put it back. Then she lifted him onto her shoulder. Her heart raced as she went downstairs. She had to find somewhere secret to use her ring.

She looked around hurriedly and saw the small door underneath the stairs that led to the royal broom closet. Checking to be sure that no one was watching, she dashed inside, switched on the light, and closed the door behind her.

Isabella only came in here if she was playing hide-and-seek with the maids. It was full of brooms and mops and ironing boards. Petro looked all around, his little face confused.

"No, we're not hiding, Petro," said Isabella. "I just wanted somewhere private to use my ring." She smiled as she looked at the yellow topaz ring on her finger.

One of the most exciting things about being a Rescue Princess was the magic rings Lottie had given them when they'd first met. The rings had come from Lottie's older sister, Emily, who had once been a Rescue Princess, too. The girls had promised to call one another as soon as they found an animal that needed rescuing, and now Isabella had found a whole rain forest that was in danger!

Petro's quick eyes noticed what she was looking at. He darted down her arm and tapped on the yellow topaz with his little fingers.

"No, Petro!" Isabella laughed, covering the jewel with her other hand so that he couldn't touch it. "This ring lets me call the other princesses. You can't use it."

Carefully, she pressed the yellow topaz and held her breath. The jewel lit up brightly, sending a yellow glow across the walls of the closet.

Isabella raised her hand and spoke clearly into the jewel. "I have a message for the Rescue Princesses! This is Isabella. I need you to come and help the animals of the rain forest. I've persuaded my mom to invite you to visit."

She paused. She could hear faint noises through the jewel.

"Hello! This is Lottie!" came the reply. "That's great work, Isabella. See you soon!"

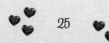

25

"This is Rosalind!" said a second voice. "I'm glad we're doing another rescue at last, I was starting to wonder if anything would happen."

There was a gentle cough and a third voice came through. "Thanks for calling me, Isabella. This is Amina and I can't wait to see you!"

"Bye!" called Isabella. "See you all soon!" The yellow topaz jewel stopped glowing and she hugged Petro excitedly. She couldn't wait for the other princesses to get here!

CHAPTER FOUR

The Treasure Hunters

Isabella sneaked out of the royal broom closet with flushed cheeks and sparkling eyes. How long would it take for the other princesses to arrive? She hoped it wouldn't be too long! She went into the dining room to see if there was any lunch left. Petro bounded onto the table and began picking bananas out of the fruit bowl.

Isabella was about to help herself to a sandwich from a silver dish when suddenly she heard an engine roaring, and a large orange truck drove up to the front door. She went over to look out the window. The truck stopped and a group of men climbed out. The king came hurrying down the front steps to meet them. Then they all went inside.

Isabella frowned deeply. She was sure they were the same men she'd seen cutting down the trees. Why were they here? She tiptoed down the hallway. Hearing voices inside her dad's study, she went closer and looked through a gap in the door.

She could see her dad sitting down at his desk with the scroll he'd shown her at lunchtime spread out in front of him. The visitors were sitting across the desk.

"Thank you for seeing us, Your Majesty." The man who spoke had a square face and a black moustache.

"What is it, Mr. Madelo?" said the king eagerly. "Have you found the gold?"

"No, we haven't found it yet, but we're very close now," replied the square-faced man. "That's why we're here. We need to look at the Silken Scroll again, to work out the next part of the secret code."

"Yes, yes, of course!" said King Victor impatiently. "Here it is." He passed them the scroll and they all crowded around to look at it more closely.

"Hmm . . ." Mr. Madelo looked at the crinkled, yellowy scroll. "This part of the code is difficult. . . ." He traced a finger across the words on the paper and frowned.

"But can you figure it out?" asked the king anxiously.

"Of course!" Mr. Madelo smiled. "I have been breaking codes for many years. The gold will soon be mine . . . I mean, ours!"

"That's excellent!" cried the king.

Mr. Madelo stood up and bowed. "We will return when we have more news for you."

Isabella stared at them through the crack in the door, her heart thumping. These men were about to start cutting down even more forest trees. She had to think of something fast!

She flung the study door open, putting a wide smile on her face. "Good afternoon! Can I offer you some coffee and cake?"

The men looked startled. "Er . . . well . . ." began Mr. Madelo. "That's very nice of you but —"

"It's our custom here in Belatina to offer guests something to eat," she said hopefully. "We wouldn't want you to go away hungry."

King Victor sighed. "I suppose that's true. Thank you for reminding me,

Isabella. Please tell Cook to send some refreshments in."

Isabella beamed and skipped along to the kitchens to find Josefina, their cook. "Josefina! Can we have some coffee and cake for my dad's visitors, please? And can I help you?"

Josefina, who was a short woman with a wide smile, put her apron on. "Of course you can, Princess Isabella! I baked a big chocolate cake this morning. You can get some plates and slice it up for me."

Isabella took the plates from the cupboard, sliced up the cake, and set it all out on a tray. Then she carried the tray to her dad's study and Josefina followed her with the coffee. The cake looked delicious with its thick, chocolatey icing, but Isabella didn't take a slice. She wanted to save it all for the treasure hunters, because if they had seconds it would take them even longer to go back to the rain forest. Then they would have even less time to chop down trees before nighttime came!

Josefina returned to the kitchen and the men ate hungrily. Isabella's feeling of triumph faded as she watched them. They were eating too fast! They would be finished in a minute. The sun shone through the study window. It was still high in the sky, which meant there were hours to go until sunset.

Isabella raced back to the kitchen. "Josefina! I don't think these visitors come from our kingdom. Are there any local recipes that we can offer them?" She looked pleadingly at the cook.

"They can try my special banana-nut bread, and after that they can have some mango ice cream," said Josefina. "Let me see what else I've got!"

Isabella took plates of the banana-nut bread to the king's study. "Our cook will be so pleased if you try this!" she said breathlessly. "I'll go get the mango ice cream, and we have a special toffee sauce as well!"

After trying three more dishes, the men leaned back in their chairs, clutching their stomachs.

"Would you like some more ice cream?" asked Isabella eagerly. "Or can I get you some lemonade?"

"I'm really full," said Mr. Madelo, wiping cake crumbs off his moustache.

"But please have something else —" began Isabella.

King Victor got up from his chair. "That's enough, Isabella. You've been very kind to our guests, but these men have a job to do." He led the treasure hunters to the front steps. "Let me know as soon as you find anything."

"We will, Your Majesty," said Mr. Madelo.

Isabella watched sadly as the treasure hunters climbed back into their truck.

"Wait a minute!" said one of the men. "Where are the keys? I left them right here next to the steering wheel."

The men checked in their pockets and then searched the truck, but they couldn't find the keys anywhere.

"Maybe you left them in my study?" suggested the king, hurrying back inside to look. But he came back empty-handed.

The men stood on the front steps of the palace, looking confused. "Surely someone wouldn't have taken them?" said Mr. Madelo.

"Isabella, do you know where they are?" asked the king.

"No, I haven't seen them," said Isabella truthfully. She gazed around the palace garden, suddenly realizing that she hadn't seen Petro since the treasure hunters arrived, and he usually spent most of the time by her side.

Then she spotted him and put her hand over her mouth to stop a giggle. Petro was dancing around on the smooth stone edge of the palace fountain. When he saw her watching, he jumped down from the fountain's edge and galloped away through the flower beds.

"We need our truck," said Mr. Madelo. "Our equipment is much too heavy to carry."

"Go get everyone in the palace," King Victor told the guards at the front door. "We must find the keys."

The next two hours were spent hunting all around the palace and the gardens for the truck keys. Everyone came to help except Josefina, who said she had too much baking to do to spare the time. Everyone got hot and tired, and the sun dipped toward the tops of the trees.

Petro galloped over to Isabella as she searched another flower bed. She was secretly delighted that the keys were lost, although she was sorry that it was making everyone else so upset.

"Petro, did you take the keys from the truck?" she whispered.

Petro leapt onto her shoulder and chattered into her ear.

"Hold on!" called the king, looking into the fountain. "I think I see something shiny in here." He rolled up the sleeve of his royal robe, plunged his hand into the water, and lifted up the dripping keys. "At last! I found them!"

"Thank you, Your Majesty!" Mr. Madelo bowed as he took the keys. "It's too late to carry on our search for the treasure today, because it will get dark soon. We'll start again tomorrow morning."

The treasure hunters drove away and Isabella hid a smile as she and Petro walked back into the palace.

"Isabella!" her mom called. "Did Petro take the keys? He can be a little naughty sometimes!"

"I don't know," said Isabella truthfully. "I didn't see him take them."

As the queen turned away, Isabella whispered to Petro. "I bet it was you and I don't think it was naughty at all! I think it was very, very smart!"

CHAPTER FIVE

The Palace of Belatina

Isabella got up really early the next morning, hoping to find out when the other princesses would arrive. She was rushing downstairs to ask her mom about it when she heard the sound of a car driving up outside, followed by girls' voices. Petro, who was swinging from the banister, pricked up his ears.

"Can they really be here already, Petro?" Isabella trembled with excitement as she yanked open the front door.

Three princesses were climbing the steps. Leading the way was Lottie, with her green eyes and tight red curls, wearing a crimson dress. Behind them, their maids began unloading suitcases from the car.

"Hello! Did you miss us?" Lottie grinned and hugged Isabella.

"Yes, I did! I'm so happy to see you!" said Isabella. "How did you get here so quickly?"

"We all caught planes that flew overnight," explained Amina, smiling. Her long black hair hung over a turquoise dress that was fastened at one shoulder. "I've never flown during the nighttime before. I slept most of the way."

"At least you didn't have to come from the kingdom of Dalvia like I did," groaned Rosalind, trying to shake the creases from her blue dress. "It took a long time to get here."

"Luckily, our planes landed at around the same time," Amina told Isabella. "And now we can't wait to help your rain-forest animals!"

"Come and have some breakfast first," said Isabella. "You must be really hungry." She looked around for Petro as she led them inside. She really wanted the princesses to meet him, but she couldn't see him anywhere.

When they'd eaten breakfast, Queen Neva swept into the room. "Welcome to the palace of Belatina, Princesses!"

"Thank you so much for inviting us to visit," said Amina.

"Thank you," said Lottie and Rosalind, and they all curtsied.

"You're welcome, girls," said Queen Neva with a smile. "Isabella will love having you here. You can do some great princess things together!" She looked doubtfully at Lottie's messy red curls. "Maybe you would all like to unpack and freshen up a little?"

"I'll help them take their suitcases upstairs," said Isabella hastily.

"Very well," said her mom.

Isabella showed her friends their rooms, which were on the top floor of the palace, next to her own. Then they met up in her bedroom to talk.

"You have to tell us what the animal emergency is!" cried Lottie. "If I have to wait any longer to find out, I'm going to burst!"

Isabella sat down under the yellow canopy of her huge four-poster bed and the others gathered around her. "It all started yesterday, when Petro and I heard a loud noise in the rain forest. When we went to look, we found out that there are men hunting for treasure and they're cutting down trees to make space to dig. They don't care how many forest creatures they hurt or that they've cut down some of the monkeys' favorite fruit trees." Her eyes filled with tears at the thought of it.

"Oh no! That's awful!" Amina gasped.

"How horrible!" Lottie's eyes flashed.

"Who's Petro?" said Rosalind.

"Oh! I forgot you hadn't seen him yet!" Isabella looked around, but there was still no sign of her monkey. "I really want you to meet him." She got up and opened her bedroom door. "Petro! Where are you?" she called down the corridor.

"Is he your brother?" asked Lottie.

"Or a cousin?" said Amina.

"No!" Isabella laughed. "Petro isn't a boy at all!"

There was a chattering sound near

the window. Then the curtains moved strangely.

Rosalind leapt off the bed, her eyes wide. "Isabella! I think there's something spooky near your window!"

Isabella rushed over and peeked around the edge of the yellow drapes. A little brown face with big eyes stared back at her. "Petro! Come out! It's not like you to be so shy."

Petro dangled from the curtains for a moment, then he leapt down to Isabella's shoulder. She stroked his head lovingly.

"Oh! He's a monkey!" cried Lottie, and the girls began to laugh.

"This is Petro. I found him all alone in the forest when he was a baby," explained Isabella. "I brought him back here and took care of him. We've been best friends ever since."

"You're so lucky!" said Rosalind. "I have two dogs, three cats, and a hamster, but I don't have a monkey." She gently rubbed Petro's furry ears. Amina and Lottie came over to stroke him, too. Petro curled his tail around his toes and chattered a friendly greeting.

"See! There was nothing to be afraid of," Isabella said to Petro. "Monkeys aren't really supposed to be kept as pets," she told the princesses, "but Petro can go back into the rain forest whenever he wants. Usually we go together! I think of him as more of a friend than a pet."

"But what about all the other monkeys — the ones whose trees are being cut down?" Lottie reminded them. "We should start planning how to help them."

"Your mom and dad won't tell the men to stop chopping down the trees?" Amina asked Isabella.

Isabella shook her head. "I've tried to talk to my parents about it already."

"Why don't we scare the treasure hunters away!" suggested Rosalind excitedly. "We could sneak up on them using our ninja moves and then frighten them."

"There are a lot of them, so I don't think they'll get scared that easily," said Isabella.

Rosalind pouted. "Well, I thought it was a good idea."

"What is it that they're looking for?" asked Amina.

"Some lost gold that was hidden in the forest a long time ago." Isabella sighed. "That's what they want. I just wish they didn't have to hurt the trees and animals to find it."

Amina looked thoughtful. "Why don't we find it first? Then they have no reason to keep doing what they're doing."

"It would certainly teach them a lesson," said Rosalind.

"How are we going to do that, though?" said Lottie.

"I know! My dad's got the Silken Scroll in his study," said Isabella. "It's like an ancient treasure map that explains how to find the gold, and the clues are written in a secret code. If we can figure out the code, it will tell us what to do!"

CHAPTER SIX

Ninja Outfits

"Let's go downstairs right now and see if we can get a peek at the scroll!" said Isabella, her eyes shining.

"Just a minute!" said Lottie. "I brought something that might help with our adventures. I'll go get it."

"I brought something, too," said Rosalind. "It's in my suitcase." Both girls rushed out of the room.

Isabella and Amina looked at each

other. "Do you know what they're talking about?" asked Isabella.

Amina shook her head.

Rosalind returned first, carrying a blue bag made from a soft, velvety material. "I've been thinking about the ninja moves that we used when we rescued those horses a few weeks ago," she said breathlessly. "I decided that we needed some ninja outfits that were suitable for different places. I got my maid to help me make them."

"Wow, Rosalind!" said Isabella. "I can't believe you did all that!"

Rosalind looked pleased. "These are the ones I made for doing ninja moves in a forest." She pulled a collection of dark green T-shirts and leggings from the bag and held them up to show the others.

"You're really into using ninja moves, aren't you?" said Amina.

Rosalind nodded. "I've been practicing a lot. I'd really like to find that lost book, *The Book of Ninja*, that has every single ninja move inside it." She stopped suddenly when the door swung open, but it was only Lottie returning with a large golden box.

"Those look great!" said Lottie, looking at Rosalind's ninja outfits. "We'll really be camouflaged among the trees wearing green."

Rosalind put the clothes down. "What did you bring?" she asked curiously.

"Remember how I told you that my sister and her friends used to rescue animals, and how they shaped magic jewels to help them?" said Lottie. "Well, my sister gave me this box so that we could try making them ourselves!"

She opened the golden box and showed them a collection of small silver tools.

Then she opened a hidden drawer underneath to reveal a collection of jewels in every shape, size, and color. Rubies, sapphires, emeralds, and diamonds all sparkled in the morning light.

"Amazing!" Amina gasped. "Your sister is really nice, Lottie."

Lottie shrugged. "She's OK sometimes, I guess. There are some instructions about how to use the tools. I thought we could try later."

"That would be awesome!" Isabella shook her curly brown hair, her eyes shining. "Let's put on the ninja outfits right now and then go downstairs to look at the treasure map. After that we'll be ready to go into the forest."

"Let's take a backpack with us, too," said Lottie. "We might need water and snacks later on."

Through the window came the distant sounds of banging and sawing.

"That's probably the treasure hunters. They're cutting down another tree already," said Isabella. "Let's hurry."

The princesses quickly changed into the green T-shirts and leggings, while Petro leapt around the room excitedly and dangled from the lampshade.

Lottie borrowed Isabella's backpack and packed it with food, drinks, and some of the jewel-making tools. Then she put it on her back. When they were all ready, Rosalind opened the bedroom door a tiny crack. "There's no one out here," she whispered. "I think it's safe to go!"

"Now remember, Petro, don't give us away!" Isabella put a finger to her lips to show the little monkey that he should be quiet. Petro sprang onto her shoulder and obediently put his hand over his mouth.

Together, they sneaked along the corridor to the top of the stairs and looked down. The hallway was empty and the palace seemed really quiet. Isabella led them down the stairs and over to the door of her dad's study.

She listened for a moment. There was no sound from inside, so she crept in and hurried over to her dad's desk.

"Is the scroll there?" asked Rosalind.

"I can't see it," said Isabella. "But maybe my dad hid it in one of the drawers."

Lottie closed the door and put her ear to it. "I'll stand here and listen in case anyone comes along."

There were three drawers in the desk. Isabella bent down to open the first one, and accidentally knocked over the chair behind her. It fell to the floor with a loud *thump*. "Sorry!" she said. "I didn't mean to do that."

Rosalind sighed. "We'll have to hurry now. Someone might come to find out what the noise was."

"I'll be quick." Isabella flushed deeply and opened the first drawer, but it only had pens and pencils inside it. Amina looked in the second drawer, but that was full of blank paper. Then Isabella pulled open the last drawer and instantly recognized the scroll, which was rolled up and fastened with an elastic band.

"I got it!" She grinned. Gently, she pulled off the band and unrolled the paper, which was yellow with age and crinkled at the edges.

"I can't wait to see the secret code!" said Rosalind.

The scroll was covered with writing and had a small picture in the middle. Isabella's heart sank. The paper was so

old that the words were hard to read. What if she couldn't even make out what the letters were?

Just then, Lottie waved her hand for them to be quiet. There was a noise in the corridor.

"Where have those princesses gone?" said Queen Neva, her footsteps coming closer. "Have you seen them, Josefina?"

"No, I haven't, Your Majesty," came Josefina's reply.

"That's very strange, because the guards say they haven't gone outside and yet I can't find them in any of the rooms," Queen Neva went on. "I was just about to ask them if they wanted to learn the history of our royal crowns and tiaras. I wonder if there's anywhere I haven't looked."

The girls held their breaths as the

queen's footsteps came even closer. Isabella stared at the door anxiously. What would her mom say if she caught them all in here, searching the king's desk and wearing strange green ninja outfits?

Then, just as she expected her mom to burst in, a faint chattering noise started.

"What's that?" Queen Neva's voice was right outside the door. "Petro, what's that shiny thing that you're holding? Have you been in my room and taken something from my jewelry box? Come back at once!" Her footsteps sped up, but grew fainter.

Lottie opened the door a tiny crack. "Petro saved us! The queen followed him upstairs."

Isabella carefully rolled up the Silken Scroll and put the elastic band back on.

"Let's go quickly, before my mom comes back!"

They tiptoed down the hallway and out the front door, then ran across the garden toward the rain forest.

CHAPTER SEVEN

The Silken Scroll

The princesses ran through the front gate, only slowing down once they reached the trees. A brown shape came bounding across the palace garden to join them.

Isabella called to the little monkey. "Petro! You were such a star, you kept us from being caught!"

"What is he holding?" asked Lottie.

Petro swung over the palace gate and jumped down to the ground. Something blue and sparkly gleamed in his hand.

"Come here, Petro." Isabella knelt and beckoned him closer. He bounced over to her and she took a butterfly hair clip from his grasp. It was the one with the sapphire wings that he had been playing with the day before.

"Oh, dear! You shouldn't have taken this," Isabella told him. "It's not yours."

"Who does it belong to?" asked Rosalind.

"It's from my mom's jewelry box, and it's very special." Isabella held the butterfly-shaped hair clip out to show them. The sapphire jewels on its wings shone a beautiful deep blue. "We'll have to return it, but let's find the treasure first; there's no time to lose." She handed the hair clip to Lottie, who put it away safely in the backpack on her shoulder.

The princesses ran into the rain forest. Isabella led the way along the paths she knew so well. Lottie, Amina, and

Rosalind followed her, staring in amazement at the brightly colored parrots and the toucans with their golden beaks.

"Wow!" said Lottie. "Look at that red frog; I've never seen one as bright as that before."

"And look! Aren't they cute?" Rosalind pointed at a troop of small monkeys swinging through the trees at top speed. One was carrying a tiny baby on its back.

"They look as if something scared them." Isabella bit her lip. "I bet they're running away from the treasure hunters with their axes and saws." She unrolled the scroll. "Horrible men! We *must* figure out where the gold is before they do."

The girls crowded around the paper, which had rough edges and cracks running across it. The writing was squiggly and the ink was faded, but as they stared at it they began to make out what it said.

"Look! Here are the symbols for north, south, east, and west," said Amina.

"And the picture in the middle shows us where the river is." Isabella pointed at a curved line running across the small picture. "The palace isn't on here, but I guess that's because this scroll was written before the palace was even built."

"Where's the hidden treasure, though?" said Rosalind.

Isabella squinted at the letters. They were long and curly, which made them hard to read, and splotches and cracks covered parts of some of the letters. "'I live in the . . . forest.'" She read the first line haltingly. "Ooh, how funny! They made the dot on top of the letter I into a monkey's face!"

"There's a monkey's face on every

line — look!" Lottie pointed to the little monkey faces. "It looks like they're above certain letters."

"What do the other lines say?" demanded Rosalind.

"Just a minute, some of the words are hard to see because the paper is so old."

Isabella took a deep breath and read:

I live in the forest

I am small and funny.

I swing high and low

Loving the shady trees

With their branches and leaves

And delicious fruit.

What am I?

"It's a riddle," said Lottie. "I think it's describing an animal."

"I think so, too," agreed Amina. "An animal that's small and funny."

Petro leapt onto Isabella's shoulder, chattering loudly. Isabella laughed. "Petro knows what the animal is!"

"Of course!" said Lottie. "Small and funny — it's a monkey!"

"But how does that help us find the gold?" said Rosalind. "Does it mean that the monkeys know where the treasure is?"

"No, they can't! It was hidden too long ago," said Isabella, frowning.

The princesses all looked puzzled. "Let's keep walking and look for clues," said Lottie at last. "Maybe the picture will help us."

As they walked, the sounds of banging and sawing grew louder, and they could hear the treasure hunters shouting to one another. The ground sloped down to a wide river with trees all the way along the banks.

There was more noise from the treasure hunters up ahead. Isabella put a finger to her lips and beckoned to the others. They hid behind a tree with a wide trunk and peered out. They could see the treasure hunters standing next to two fallen trees not far from the riverbank.

"There's no sign of the gold here," said one man. "Are you sure we're looking in the right place?"

"I have no idea!" replied Mr. Madelo. "It must be around here somewhere."

"But you told the king you'd cracked the code on the scroll," said another man.

"Of course I've cracked it!" said Mr. Madelo. "It's just a crummy old piece of paper with a silly riddle that means monkey. That doesn't help us at all.

We just have to keep cutting down trees until we find something." He aimed a kick at one of the fallen trees.

"What a waste of two beautiful trees," whispered Lottie.

"And how terrible for all the creatures that lived in them," said Amina.

Isabella's eyes flashed. "I'm sure there is a real clue somewhere on the Silken Scroll, and we're going to find it! We *won't* let them destroy this amazing forest!"

CHAPTER EIGHT

Monkey Island

Isabella stared at the Silken Scroll again. "The riddle does mean monkey," she muttered. "But maybe the little faces mean something, too."

"You mean the monkey faces?" said Amina. "Do you think they're above certain letters for a reason?"

"I think we should keep walking and look for clues in the forest," said Rosalind. "I'm glad the treasure hunters haven't chopped down those trees. See all the monkeys living there?"

Rosalind pointed at a group of trees on the other side of the river. They were full of monkeys jumping from branch to branch and chattering to one another. Petro watched them closely, as if he was ready to leap away and join them.

"That's actually a little island in the middle of the river," Isabella told her. "Lots of monkeys like living there. I guess they feel safe." Her eyes suddenly widened as she stared at the scroll in her hand. "Hold on! The monkey face on the first line is above the letter I. Then on line two it's by an S, then an L, then A, N, D."

"So it's I-S-L-A-N-D," said Lottie thoughtfully. "The answer to the riddle is monkey."

"It's Monkey Island!" they burst out

together. Then they had to duck down
to hide as the treasure hunters turned in
their direction.

"What was that noise?" asked one man.

"Probably another silly parrot," said
Mr. Madelo. "Come on now, get back
to work."

"The lost gold must be on Monkey
Island," whispered Isabella as soon as
the men had turned away. "It must have
been there all this time!"

"But how do we get across? Is there a
bridge?" asked Rosalind.

Isabella shook her head. "Either we
have to swing across like Petro or make a
bridge ourselves."

"Let's swing," whispered Amina, but the
others shook their heads.

"I'd rather use a bridge," said Lottie. "I'd
be a lot less likely to fall in."

"One of those fallen trees would make a good bridge. It's too bad they're too heavy for us to carry," said Rosalind.

"But we might be able to lift that big branch over there." Isabella pointed at a sturdy branch that had broken off one of the fallen trees. "Look, the men are going back to their truck. If we're quick we could get the branch right now. Then we could cross to the island without them ever seeing us."

The princesses sneaked forward, glad that they were camouflaged in their green ninja clothes. The treasure hunters were standing next to their truck not far away. From the clashes and clanks, it sounded as if they were unloading more tools.

Isabella raced to one end of the branch, while Lottie stood at the other end and Rosalind and Amina went in the middle.

"Ready, everyone?" whispered Isabella. Together, they all heaved the branch up.

"It's heavy!" Amina gasped.

"Quick, before they come back!" hissed Lottie.

Isabella looked at the treasure hunters, but luckily they were still busy by the truck. Her arms began to ache as she led the way down to the riverbank. Her foot caught on a tree root and she nearly lost her balance. Holding the branch tightly, she told herself to be careful. She couldn't ruin everything by falling over.

"Let's go a little farther," muttered Lottie. "We need to be sure that those men can't see what we're doing."

They trudged along the bank until they found a place where the river was narrow and they were hidden from view by the trees.

"But how are we going to lay the

branch across so that it makes an actual bridge?" asked Amina.

"It would be easier if one of us could swing across and catch it on the other side." Isabella smiled at Amina. "Do you think you could do that? You are better at gymnastics than the rest of us!"

"I'll try!" Amina said. She climbed a tree that stretched out over the water and managed to swing across to the opposite bank. Petro followed her, chattering excitedly.

"That was perfect!" said Lottie. "Are you ready to catch the branch?"

Amina pushed back her long dark hair. "Yes, ready," she said.

Petro dangled from a tree by his tail, enjoying the whole adventure.

Together, Isabella, Lottie, and Rosalind heaved the branch across the river. It was hard work, and Isabella began to worry that the branch might fall in and sink below the water. At last they pushed it across. Amina grabbed it on the other side and dragged it into place.

Isabella put one foot on the thick branch and it wobbled frantically. How would she ever manage to get across? She found it hard just to keep her balance.

"Keep going and don't look down," advised Lottie.

Isabella held her breath as she tiptoed across, her arms stretched out on either side. Right in the middle, the branch trembled again and she thought she was going to fall in. But she kept going until she was safely on the opposite bank.

"Well done!" whispered Amina, squeezing her hand.

Isabella grinned. "Thanks."

Petro dropped down onto her shoulder and nuzzled her ear.

One by one, Lottie and Rosalind crossed the river. When they were all safely on the other side, Isabella unfurled the Silken Scroll again. A group of monkeys swung down from the treetops and stared curiously at the girls. Petro leapt from Isabella's shoulder into the branches to play with them.

"Look!" Isabella turned the scroll over. "There are two more lines of writing on the other side." Just then, the sounds of banging and sawing started up again. "Oh! Those men are cutting down another tree. We have to hurry!"

"Let me try," said Amina calmly. "I think the first line says: 'Find the tallest tree.'"

"Well, that should be easy! Let's find it right now." Isabella led the way, crashing through some bushes and making a long-snouted animal run away in fear.

"What is that?" Rosalind stared
wide-eyed at the dark, piglike creature.

"It's a tapir," said Isabella. "Don't
worry, it won't hurt you."

"Wasn't the scroll written a long time
ago?" said Lottie, frowning. "Maybe the
tall tree they were talking about has
fallen down since then."

"Some of the trees in this rain forest are
hundreds of years old," said Isabella. "So
it might still be here."

"How about that one!" cried Amina,
pointing at a huge tree whose branches
soared far above the others.

They rushed over and gazed up at its
thick trunk.

Isabella's heart was racing. "What does
the last line of writing say?" she asked
breathlessly.

" 'Look in the heart of the tree and you

will find the gold,' " Amina read slowly. "I don't really understand that part."

" 'The heart of the tree,' " echoed Isabella. "I wonder where that is?" She walked all around the trunk, looking at every mark and crack in the wood.

"Everyone get behind the tree!" hissed Lottie. "There's a man looking across at the island."

They all hid behind the tree. The treasure hunter walked along the riverbank and noticed the branch they'd laid across the river as a bridge. He scratched his head.

"I hope he doesn't cross over," muttered Isabella, "because if he does we're in really big trouble!"

CHAPTER NINE

Rain-Forest Treasure

The princesses watched the man for several minutes as he looked at their bridge and stared across at the island. At last he wandered back toward the other men.

"That was close," muttered Lottie. "I don't think he saw us."

"But where are we supposed to look for the gold? Maybe we have to climb up the tree?" suggested Rosalind.

"The scroll says *the heart of the tree,*

and I think that really means the roots."
Isabella crouched down to look at the
base of the tree. The roots jutted out of
the ground and there were gaps between
them. She caught a glimpse of something
hidden in there.

"I can see something!" She reached
into the hollow between two roots and
dragged out an old leather bag with a
strap covered in red beads. A couple of
beads fell off it and rolled away. The bag
felt really heavy, and something jingled
inside it.

"Let's see what's in there," said
Rosalind excitedly.

Isabella undid the straps and a bright
glow burst from the bag. She put her
hand in and took out a small golden
statue. "Look at this! It's beautiful!"

"That's amazing!" Amina reached in
and pulled out a handful of gold coins.

Lottie reached into the bag and took out a large golden mask in the shape of a monkey's head. "Wow! This treasure is awesome!"

"Let's take everything back to the palace," said Isabella. "Once we've shown this to my dad, he can tell the men to stop hunting for the treasure. Then all the trees and creatures will be safe again."

But as she stood up, a shout came from across the water. The treasure hunters were standing on the edge of the river and looking right at them.

"Hey!" shouted one. "What are you girls doing with our gold?"

"They saw us! What should we do?" said Amina.

"We have to get across the river and back to the palace as fast as we can!" said Lottie.

Isabella tried to lift up the old leather

bag, but she couldn't. "I can't move this; the gold is too heavy!"

"Let's all lift it together." Lottie's green eyes were determined.

They all grabbed the bag, but it still didn't move.

A yell came from across the river. "Hey! Put that gold back or you'll be sorry!" It was Mr. Madelo, his black moustache twitching. He turned to the other men. "Find a way to get over to that island and take the gold from them!"

The men ran along the riverbank toward the branch that the girls had used as a bridge.

"Rosalind! Amina!" hissed Isabella. "Try to get rid of the bridge we made. See if you can push it into the water."

Rosalind and Amina dashed to the water's edge.

Startled by all the shouting, the monkeys in the treetops began calling loudly to one another.

"What are we going to do?" Isabella asked Lottie. "Even without the branch bridge those men will find a way over here. The gold's too heavy for us to move. Why should they get the treasure after all the bad things they've done?"

"Give up the gold right now!" bellowed Mr. Madelo. "Or we will cut down every single tree on that island."

Isabella's heart sank. The island's trees were home to so many monkeys. What if they got hurt?

Lottie's face turned as red as her curls. "We won't give up!" she said fiercely. "There must be a way to stop them!" She took off her backpack and looked inside it.

"What about these jewel-crafting tools?" Isabella reached into the backpack and pulled out a small chisel.

"But I didn't put any jewels in the backpack and there are only gold things in that treasure bag," said Lottie.

"How about the butterfly hair clip that Petro took from my mom's room?" said Isabella, rummaging inside the backpack to find it. "It's made from sapphires. Maybe we can use that."

There was a loud splash and a cheer from Amina and Rosalind as they managed to push the branch bridge into the water. The treasure hunters stood on the opposite bank, glaring angrily.

Lottie took some scribbled instructions from the bottom of the backpack. "This tells us how to make a jewel glow or how to make it heat up, but that won't help us."

Isabella put down the tools and picked up a tiny pot. "What does this do?"

"It's some kind of polish," said Lottie. "I can't see how that would help us, either."

Bang! An earsplitting noise made the girls jump. One of the treasure hunters was chopping down a tree right next to the river.

"We'll make our own bridge using this tree!" shouted Mr. Madelo. "Then we're coming over there to get our treasure!"

Suddenly, Isabella noticed a baby monkey clinging to the tree they were chopping down. "Stop!" she yelled to them. "There's a baby monkey right at the top of that tree. You'll hurt him if you keep going!"

But the men ignored her, their sharp axes cutting into the trunk. The tree wobbled and the tiny monkey swayed with it. His eyes were round with fear as he held tight to his branch and looked down at the treasure hunters below. The girls gasped. They had to help him somehow.

CHAPTER TEN

The Butterfly Hair Clip

"The poor thing!" said Isabella. "He must have been left behind when the other monkeys got scared and ran away."

"How can we help him?" cried Lottie. "We're so far away across the river."

"I don't know!" Isabella stared at the jeweled hair clip and the jewel-making tools strewn around her. Desperately, she pulled the lid off the pot of polish and looked at the silver cream inside.

She took some of the polish and

smeared it onto the sapphire wings of the butterfly hair clip. It glittered for a moment before disappearing. Then suddenly, the hair clip began to feel incredibly light. The sapphire wings flapped gently and the whole hair clip rose up into the air and hovered just above her hand.

"That's amazing!" Lottie gasped. "Did the polish make it do that?"

"Yes! All I did was put some on the jewels," said Isabella.

The butterfly hair clip flitted playfully from side to side, its blue wings fluttering.

"Lottie! Let's put all the treasure back into the leather bag," said Isabella. "I have an idea!"

"Really? What is it?" Lottie stuffed the gold statue, the coins, and the monkey mask into the bag, just as Amina and Rosalind ran back to them.

"Wow!" Rosalind gasped. "The hair clip is flying!"

"The polish I brought in the backpack made it do that," said Lottie.

"All we need to do now is fasten the hair clip to the bag," said Isabella. "Then maybe it will carry the whole bag away."

"That is a really strange plan," said Rosalind. "I like it! But do we have any string to tie it on with?"

"Here! Use my hair tie." Amina took it out of her pocket and handed it over.

Isabella gently grasped the flying butterfly hair clip and looped the hair tie around it. Then she twisted the other end around the bag's red beaded handle so that the butterfly still had space to flap its wings. The jeweled creature struggled for a moment, then it flew up, lifting the whole bag with it.

"It's magical!" Amina gasped.

The bag soared up through the leaves.

"It's working!" Isabella bit her lip. "I wish it would fly right over to the baby monkey, then he could catch a ride. . . ."

But just then, a furry brown shape came swinging through the branches. Petro had seen Isabella fasten the butterfly hair clip to the bag. His little eyes gleamed and he sprang forward, catching on to the bag and clinging on.

"No, Petro!" called Isabella.

But it was too late.

The bag with the gold, pulled by the sapphire butterfly, went floating up. Petro dangled underneath it with a very surprised look on his furry face. It looked like he was holding on to a balloon. Up and up went the bag. It left the island behind and went flying across the river.

The treasure hunters were talking among themselves and looking over at the island. None of them had spotted the flying bag of treasure.

"Fly across to the baby monkey!" Isabella called softly, and the butterfly changed direction, heading toward the right tree as if it could understand her.

"I think it heard you," said Rosalind. "Try it again!"

"Fly up a bit more! Fly right past the baby monkey!" called the princesses, more loudly this time.

Mr. Madelo glared at them, as if he wondered what they were yelling about.

The man swung his axe against the tree again. *Bang!* The tree shuddered. The baby monkey climbed to the tip of the highest branch, as if he was trying to get away from the horrible noise.

"Why doesn't he jump across to the next tree?" asked Amina, worried.

"He doesn't know what to do without his mother," said Isabella.

"Fly closer, butterfly hair clip!" shouted Lottie.

"Go over to the little monkey," called Rosalind, and the blue butterfly flew higher and higher.

The tree creaked even louder and began to tip sideways. The princesses held their breaths, their eyes fixed on the little baby monkey. But just as the tree started to fall, the bag of treasure sailed right overhead with Petro chattering happily underneath it.

"Petro!" cried Isabella. "Catch the baby monkey!"

Petro called urgently to the baby, who held out one tiny arm. Isabella was scared that the treasure bag would sail away too fast, but the baby monkey managed to jump from his branch and cling to Petro's back. The two monkeys floated away together above the treetops, underneath the bag of gold.

The men yelled furiously when they saw the precious gold sailing away into the sky.

"Fly away to the palace, blue butterfly!" Isabella called to the butterfly with the sapphire wings. "Fly to the palace right now!"

"I hope it gets there before the magic wears off!" said Lottie, looking at the writing on the pot of polish. "It says here it doesn't last for very long."

"Oh no!" cried Isabella. "Then Petro and the baby monkey would fall out of the sky with the bag of gold. They could get really hurt!"

CHAPTER ELEVEN

The Flying Treasure

Isabella watched anxiously as the
sapphire butterfly lifted the bag of gold
away over the treetops. The baby monkey
held on tight to Petro, looking much
happier than before.

The treasure hunters ran after the gold,
shouting and arguing.

"We have to get off this island and
follow them!" cried Rosalind.

"Come on," said Isabella, stuffing the
pot of polish back into the backpack. "I

know a shortcut back to the palace that the men won't know."

It took a little while to find a fallen branch long enough and straight enough to make a new bridge over the river. Amina swung across the water and helped them put the new branch in place. Then they crossed over as fast as they could. Ahead of them, they could hear the yells of the treasure hunters.

"We have to get there first!" Isabella plunged through the trees with her brown curls bouncing on her shoulders.

They rushed back to the palace of Belatina and ran through the tall gates just as Petro, the baby monkey, and the treasure bag sailed overhead. The bag was definitely lower now.

"We'll catch you, Petro!" called Isabella, running after him.

"How did you get here before us?" growled Mr. Madelo as he and the other treasure hunters arrived at the palace gates, red-faced from running. "That gold is ours! You girls have no right to take it."

"I thought you said you were going to give half of it to my dad?" said Isabella.

"Oh, we were never really going to give any to him," replied one man before the others shushed him.

The blue butterfly was dipping lower now, bringing the bag of gold with it. It flew across the palace gardens, only just missing the top of a statue. The princesses ran along behind it, their arms outstretched. The treasure hunters thundered after them.

"Get the gold!" yelled Mr. Madelo.

"Don't worry, little monkey!" cried Isabella. "I'll catch you if you fall, but please hang on if you can!"

The leather bag floated down toward the white palace. Isabella ran up the palace steps so fast that she nearly tripped. She steadied herself. She had to catch the baby monkey safely. The sapphire butterfly gave one last flap of its blue wings and then turned into a normal hair clip again.

Fixing her eyes on the little monkey, Isabella reached up for him just as the bag fell to the ground. She caught him and hugged him tight. He looked up at her with big black eyes.

"That was an awesome catch, Isabella!" said Lottie.

Petro leapt down from the bag and danced around as if he'd enjoyed flying through the air enormously. The bag of gold fell to the steps with a *clunk* just as the king came to the front door. The butterfly clip broke loose from the hair tie and landed next to the gold.

"What is all this noise?" asked the king sternly. "Good gracious, Isabella! Is that you? What funny green clothes you're wearing!"

"Yes, it's me, Dad!" Isabella kissed the little monkey on his head. His fur was soft and warm. He really was the cutest baby monkey she'd ever seen!

"Hey! Where's our treasure?" grumbled one of the men as they stumbled up the path behind the princesses. "How did they get that bag to fly?"

"Did someone say treasure?" The king's eyes lit up. "Is this the famous lost gold?" He hurried to open the bag and pulled out a handful of gold coins. "This is excellent! But who found it all?" He looked from the princesses in their ninja outfits to the treasure hunters.

"We found the treasure!" said Isabella.

"They stole it from us, Your Majesty!" said Mr. Madelo angrily, and the other men murmured in agreement. "It was supposed to be ours. . . . I mean, we were finding it for you!" He bowed.

Lottie stepped forward. "We heard these men say that they didn't really know where the gold was at all and that they would just chop down trees until they found it. So we had to find the treasure first and stop them."

"It's true, Dad!" said Isabella. "This little monkey nearly fell out of a tree that they were chopping down. Then Petro saved him!" She showed him the tiny monkey, who was holding on to her thumb with one little hand.

King Victor looked from the gold coins to the baby monkey and his face turned very red. "You princesses have been kind and caring. I'm sad to say that I've been thinking about the lost gold so much that I forgot what's really important."

"Er, Your Majesty?" said Mr. Madelo. "I can see you're busy, so we'll just take our half of the gold and go." He started to reach for the bag of treasure but one of the palace guards stopped him.

"I am more disappointed with myself than with you, Mr. Madelo," the king told him. "After all, I was the one who gave you permission to chop down the trees. But now I realize that I was wrong."

Mr. Madelo groaned. "But, King Victor —"

"This gold," the king continued, "will go toward starting a museum where everyone can learn more about the ancient people who hid it. And if you need to earn some money, you can come back first thing tomorrow to help me clear up the fallen trees and plant new ones in their places."

"Yes, Your Majesty!" The men bowed and trudged away to the palace gates, their shoulders drooping.

The princesses grinned at one another in delight.

"Can we plant some new trees in the forest, too?" asked Rosalind, her blue eyes sparkling.

"Yes, we would really love to help," added Amina.

"That's a marvelous idea. I am very pleased that you care about wildlife so much." King Victor stroked the baby monkey's head and smiled. "Now, why don't you go and ask Josefina for some fruit? This monkey looks hungry to me!" He gave the monkey one last pat before he went inside.

Isabella stooped to pick up the butterfly hair clip. Then two strong-looking palace guards came down the steps to carry away the gold.

"We'd better put this hair clip back in my mom's jewelry box right away," said Isabella, wiping the last smear of polish off its sapphire wings. "If I tried to tell my mom how it flew through the air, I don't think she would ever believe me!"

CHAPTER TWELVE

The Baby Monkey

The princesses took Petro and the baby monkey up to Isabella's bedroom and got lots of oranges, bananas, and pineapple for them to eat.

"Tomorrow morning when the sun comes up, we have to take this baby back to the rain forest and help him find his family again," said Isabella.

The other princesses nodded.

There was a knock at the door and Queen Neva came in. "Princesses!" she said, looking shocked. "The king said you were dressed very oddly and now I see what he meant. What are those strange clothes you're wearing?"

Isabella thought quickly; she couldn't tell her mom about the Rescue Princesses. No one else could ever know about that. So what could she say? Lottie gave her a warning look.

Suddenly, Isabella knew exactly what to say. She picked up her camera from her nightstand. "Well, you see, in these dark green clothes we blend in with the leaves in the forest, and that means that we don't startle the animals. Maybe I'll be able to take a picture of the Blue Morpho butterfly now that I've got these clothes to wear."

The queen seemed to accept the explanation. "Make sure you get changed now and give your hair a really good brushing," she said. "The banquet will be ready in ten minutes." She smiled before closing the door behind her.

Lottie picked up another piece of orange for the baby monkey. "It's amazing to think that the clues to finding the lost gold were in your dad's study all this time, Isabella," she said.

Rosalind stood up very suddenly, her blue eyes wide. "Do you think the lost *Book of Ninja* is in there, too, Isabella?"

Isabella shook her head. "I don't think so. I'm sure I would have seen it."

Rosalind's face fell.

"We have a really huge library in our palace in Kamala," said Amina. "And we have a special section that tells you where important books from around the world are kept."

"Can you imagine how much we could

learn from *The Book of Ninja*?" said Rosalind dreamily. "It tells you how to perform every single ninja move! You *will* look for it in your library in Kamala, won't you, Amina?"

"I'll take a really good look when I get back home," Amina promised her.

There was the sound of dishes clattering downstairs and Isabella suddenly thought about the banquet. "We'd better get dressed quickly!" she said.

The others rushed back to their own rooms. Isabella brushed her long brown curls and put on her favorite dress, a red one with wavy edges. Then she added her swirly gold tiara and a yellow topaz necklace to match her special ring.

Carefully, she picked up the baby monkey, and he snuggled into her arms. Then she went to meet the other princesses

in the corridor, with Petro scampering behind her.

Amina was already waiting at the top of the stairs. Her stomach made a rumbling sound. She clutched it and giggled. "I'm glad it's dinnertime," she said. "I'm really hungry." She swept her long black hair over her shoulders and the emerald ring on her finger sparkled. Her long turquoise dress swept down to the floor and a silver crown was perched on her head.

"Me, too!" said Rosalind. "I hope there's something good to eat!" She smoothed away the creases in her dark blue dress. On top of her blond hair, she wore a tiara with lots of tiny blue jewels that matched her sapphire ring.

Lottie came out of her room last, wearing a crimson dress. A ruby tiara rested on her tight red curls, matching her ruby ring. "That was a really exciting day." She grinned. "I think we're getting better and better at animal rescues!"

"I love being a Rescue Princess! I'm starting to think that princesses can do anything," said Amina happily. "Oh, wait! What's that funny noise?"

Petro leapt up onto the banister right next to Amina. He fixed his big black eyes on her and chattered earnestly.

Isabella laughed. "I think Petro wants you to remember it wasn't just princesses who helped this time." She smiled at him. "You're right, Petro! You're not a Rescue Princess, but you were really brave today!"

"Sorry, Petro, I didn't mean to leave you out!" Amina kissed the top of his furry head.

Petro leapt across to Amina's shoulder and nuzzled her ear, making them all laugh.

"I'm so happy that we helped keep the rain forest safe," said Isabella, hugging the baby monkey tightly. "I wonder what our next adventure will be!"

Can't wait for
the Rescue Princesses' next
animal adventure?

The Shimmering Stone

Turn the page for
a sneak peek!

CHAPTER ONE

The Royal Wedding

Princess Amina tiptoed into the palace courtyard and peered out from behind a pillar, clutching her binoculars in one hand. Her long black hair hung loosely over her turquoise dress. On her arm she wore a bracelet with a golden-brown stone that shimmered as she moved.

She looked around carefully. Rows of tables were laid out in the center of the courtyard, ready for the banquet tonight. There was nobody here. If she was quick, maybe she could reach the garden without being seen! She cast one last look around before darting out of her hiding place and running across the courtyard. She'd almost reached the other side when she ran straight into her cousin Princess Rani, and tumbled to the ground.

Rani, who was much older and taller, helped her up. "Hey!" she said, laughing. "What's the hurry? Is there a wild animal chasing you?"

"Oh, sorry, Rani! I didn't see you!" gasped Amina.

"Don't worry, I'm all right!" said Rani. "But why are you in such a rush?"

"I was looking out my bedroom window with my binoculars and I'm sure I saw a tiger outside the palace wall!" explained Amina. "It was walking through the long grass next to the river. I was just going to take a closer look." She held out her binoculars. "Oh no!" She stopped and looked at them more closely.

"What's wrong?" asked Rani.

"One of the lenses is broken. I must have knocked it against the ground when I fell." She showed her cousin the crack in the glass on one side of the binoculars. Her heart sank. She used her binoculars nearly every day. They were so handy for seeing all the Kamalan wildlife.

"What a shame!" said Rani sympathetically. "I know how much you love them. Come and show me the tiger — we can close one eye and look through the side that isn't broken."

"All right, then." Amina turned toward the archway that led out to the garden.

"Rani! Amina! Where are you?" A loud voice came from inside the palace.

Amina froze. Her aunt, Queen Keshi, had been hurrying around the palace all morning. With the royal visitors due to arrive that day, there was lots to do.

"Mom wants us," said Rani. "We'll have to look for your tiger later."

"But he might be gone by then!" Amina looked longingly at the archway. If only she could get through before her aunt came along. She wanted to see the tiger so badly!

"You go, then," said Rani. "Mom probably wants me to try on my wedding dress for the hundredth time! You should go and have some fun."

Amina grinned. Even though Rani was much older, she was a perfect cousin — kind and funny. Amina was so happy that she was going to be her bridesmaid the next day!

"There you are!" Queen Keshi climbed down the steps to the courtyard, wearing a purple sari and a gold crown.

"Rani, you must try on your wedding dress one more time. Amina, I have some jobs for you to do. The royal guests are already starting to arrive and I am determined to make this the best wedding ever held in the kingdom of Kamala!"

"But, Aunt!" began Amina. "Could I go out into the garden first because —"

Queen Keshi waved her hands. "Amina! There isn't much time! We need to get the table decorations right and then we have to make sure that the guests' rooms are ready."

Amina's shoulders drooped. She wished she could go and see the tiger first. She'd seen deer and monkeys near the palace before, but never a tiger.

Rani noticed her disappointed face.

"Maybe Amina could pick some flowers from the garden to decorate the tables?" she said. "Maybe some of those pink and white lilies."

Amina perked up. If she was picking flowers in the garden, then she could sneak a look over the wall with her binoculars at the same time. She looked hopefully at her aunt.

Queen Keshi nodded. "Just make sure you pick plenty, and *don't* forget to put them in water, so that they last until the wedding. And *don't* get dirt under your fingernails!" She swept back up the steps.

Rani gave Amina a quick grin and followed her mom.